SIMON & SCHUSTER BOOKS FOR YOUNG READERS • An imprint of Simon & Schuster Children's Publishing Division • 1230 Avenue of the Americas, New York, New York 10020 • Text © 2022 by Shelley Moore Thomas • Illustration © 2022 by Melissa Castrillón • Book design by Lizzy Bromley © 2022 by Simon & Schuster, Inc. • All rights reserved, including the right of reproduction in whole or in part in any form. • SIMON & SCHUSTER BOOKS FOR YOUNG READERS and related marks are trademarks of Simon & Schuster, Inc. • For information about special discounts for bulk purchases, please contact Simon & Schuster Special Sales at 1-866-506-1949 or business@simonandschuster.com. • The Simon & Schuster Speakers Bureau can bring authors to your live event. For more information or to book an event, contact the Simon & Schuster Speakers Bureau at 1-866-248-3049 or visit our website at www.simonspeakers.com. • The text for this book was set in Usherwood. • The illustrations for this book were rendered in graphite and colored digitally. • Manufactured in China • 0622 SCP • First Edition • 2 4 6 8 10 9 7 5 3 1 • Library of Congress Cataloging-in-Publication Data • Names: Thomas, Shelley Moore, author. | Castrillón, Melissa, illustrator. • Title: Beginning / Shelley Moore Thomas ; illustrated by Melissa Castrillón. • Description: New York : Simon & Schuster Books for Young Readers, [2022] | "A Paula Wiseman Book." • | Audience: Ages 4–8. | Audience: Grades K–1. | Summary: From a seed to a plant, an egg to a chick, or a caterpillar to a butterfly, a child and father share the cycles in nature and come to see that as each journey ends a new adventure begins. • Identifiers: LCCN 2021047448 (print) | LCCN 2021047449 (ebook) | ISBN 9781534494435 (hardcover) | ISBN 9781534494442 (ebook) • Subjects: CYAC: Life cycles (Biology)—Fiction. | Fathers and Sons—Fiction. | LCGFT: Picture books. • Classification: LCC PZ7.T369453 Be 2022 (print) | LCC PZ7.T369453 (ebook) | DDC [E]—dc23 • LC record available at https://lccn.loc.gov/2021047448 • LC ebook record available at https://lccn.loc.gov/2021047449

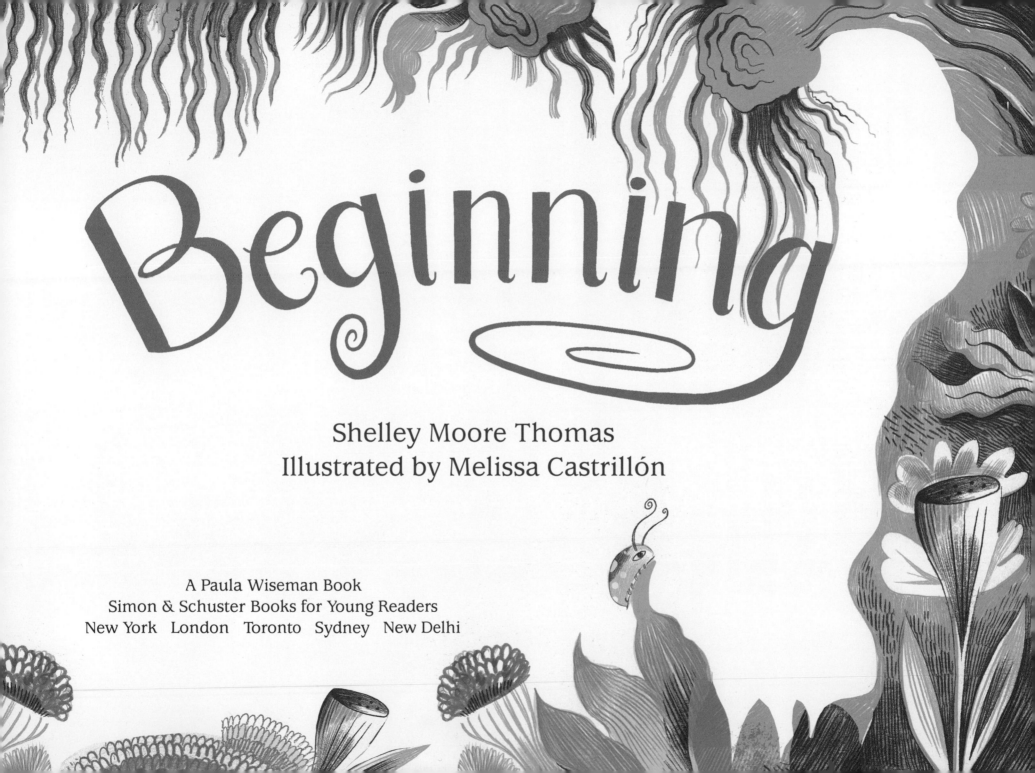

Beginning

Shelley Moore Thomas
Illustrated by Melissa Castrillón

A Paula Wiseman Book
Simon & Schuster Books for Young Readers
New York London Toronto Sydney New Delhi

The end of a seed is the beginning of a flower.

The end of an egg

is the beginning
of a chick.

The end of
a caterpillar

is the beginning
of a butterfly.

When a peach ends

a tree can begin.

When a sunrise ends
pancakes begin!

A walk ends where
the playground begins.

The end of alone

is the beginning
of together.

The end of the beach

is the beginning
of the sea.

The end of a path

is the beginning
of home.

When a sunset ends
the starlight begins.

When a
bath ends

pajamas begin.

A story ends
where dreams
begin.

The end of today

is the beginning of tomorrow,

and tomorrow,

and tomorrow.

So never fear an ending, little one.
It's all part of living, and changing,
and growing.

As each journey ends
new adventures begin.
Where will you go?
What will you be?

When this
books ends
your story
begins.